siZwe
The Chief Executive Officer

Written by **Diamond Adebowale**

Illustrations by **Busisiwe Ndlovu**

Sizwe: The Chief Executive Officer

Text © Diamond Adebowale 2017
Illustrations © Busisiwe Ndlovu 2017

This edition published in paperback in 2017 by
Verity Publishers © 2017
P. O. Box 12156 Queenswood Pretoria 0121
mail@veritypublishers.co.za
www.veritypublishers.co.za

Cover Design by Busisiwe Ndlovu

ISBN 978-1-928348-54-2

VERITY PUBLISHERS

Printed in the Republic of South Africa

sizwe

The Chief Executive Officer

VERITY PUBLISHERS

Pretoria

Sizwe and Funani were childhood friends. They both lived on the same Street in Umlazi and attended the same primary school together.

They also made friends with other boys in their school and neighbourhood, and they all played football together at school and in the park near their homes. Life was very exciting for them as little children.

One day, during one of their Life Orientation classes in Grade Seven, their teacher came into the classroom and greeted all the pupils as usual.

"Hello class!"

"Hello Teacher!" The pupils responded.

"Today, we are going to have a special class in Life Orientation," the teacher said to the learners. Then she took a piece of chalk and wrote on the blackboard, "What do you want to become in future?"

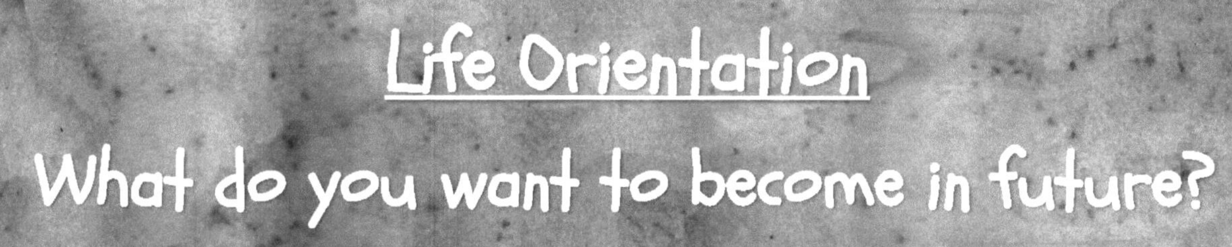

Life Orientation
What do you want to become in future?

Life Orientation
What do you want to become in future?
Lawyer = yes
*Teacher - yes
*Banker
Soldier - ok
*Trader
*Doctor
*Engineer
*Pilot

After that, the teacher took out thirty pieces of paper from her bag and placed them on the right side of her desk. Then, again, she took out thirty envelopes and placed them on the left side of her desk.

"Here on the right side of my desk are thirty pieces of plain paper, and on the left side are thirty envelopes. So, one after the other, beginning from the front row, I want each of the thirty learners in this classroom to come out and tell the class what he or she wants to become in future. After you have all told us what you want to become in future, you will then take a piece of paper from the desk and write it down. Thereafter, you will take one envelope from the left side of the desk, fold your paper neatly and seal it in the envelope. I will later tell you what to do with your envelope," the teacher concluded.

Life Orientation
What do you want to become in future?
Lawyer
Teacher
Soldier
*Doctor
*Pharmacist
*CEO

First from the front row of the class was Mbali who came out and said, "I want to be a Lawyer."

Then it was Funani's turn, and he said, "I want to be a Doctor."

Sizwe said, "I want to be a Chief Executive Officer."

Zinhle said, "I want to be a Trader."

Thabile said, "I want to be a Petroleum Engineer."

Phila said, "I want to be a Pharmacist."

Nontobeko chose to be a Dentist, while Nathi chose to be a Disk Jockey.

Sipho chose to be a Traffic Officer, and Phumzile chose to be a Politician.

Nomvula said, "I want to be a Teacher;" and Themba said, "I want to be a Soldier."

Zibuyile said, "I want to be a Banker;" and Sifiso said, "I want to be a Businessman."

Zodwa said, "I want to be an Accountant," and lastly, Bheki said, "I want to be a Pilot."

After all the learners had finished telling the class what they would like to become in future and had written it down on a piece of paper, the teacher then instructed every one of them to insert their wishes in the envelope she had given them, seal it up, and take it home.

"You are to keep the envelope in a secret place in your respective homes, and you are not allowed to open the envelope until after fifteen years when you would have completed your tertiary education, no matter the delay. Then you can confirm if your wishes for what you want to become in future had actually come true," the teacher concluded.

Sizwe was a brilliant student in High School. Sadly, he lost his parents in a motor accident when he was in Grade Eleven. Therefore, he was unable to complete his High School education. Life became hard-hitting for him without his parents. He then went to live with his uncle in KwaMashu, north of Durban. He later fled his uncle's home and became a thug in Durban beachfront.

One day, as he was wandering about the Durban beachfront without purpose, he came across his old-time classmate and friend, Funani. They both hugged each other and rejoiced at seeing each other once again. Funani also dropped out of High School, so it was easy for both of them to blend together as gangsters. They became birds of the same feather – flocking together on the breadline in Durban beachfront.

As time passes, Sizwe began to regret the hopeless life he was leading at the Durban beachfront. He was no longer enjoying leading the life of a street boy, and his mind became troubled from time to time with a feeling of sadness.

One day, Sizwe asked his friend, Funani, to accompany him to Umlazi to inquire from a soothsayer about their future.

The two boys wasted no time in telling the soothsayer why they had come to see him.

After they had narrated their stories,
the soothsayer drew two circles on the floor:
one in white ink and the other in black ink.
He dropped a millipede in-between the
two circles and said, "If the millipede crawls
into the white circle, your future will be very
successful and great; but if it crawls into the
black circle, then you are doomed! Your
future will be bleak and wretched!

As soon as the soothsayer dropped the millipede in-between the circles, it quickly began crawling towards the white circle. Sizwe and Funani were very excited.
As the millipede got to the edge of the white circle, it suddenly turned back and began crawling towards the black circle. The boys watched as the millipede moved farther away from their desired destiny to their doom. Just when the insect got to the edge of the black circle and was about entering into it, Sizwe picked it up and quickly dropped it into the white circle.

Then the soothsayer shouted and asked, "Oh no! Why did you do that?"

Sizwe simply replied by saying, "I cannot sit and watch my destiny ruined while I can still do something about it … Seeing that my destiny is in my own hands, I then decided to change its course for the better," Sizwe concluded.

"You are very correct, my dear son," said the soothsayer. "It is not in the stars to hold our destiny but in our own hands. It is truly in your moments of decision that your destiny is shaped. Go out there into the world and reshape your destiny for the better, as you have just done now," the soothsayer concluded.

Then the boys got up and left.

When they were on their way, Sizwe decided he was no longer going back to his gang at the Durban beachfront. He also advised Funani not to go back to the gangsters again, but Funani ignored his counsel and went back there.

CAR WASH

Sizwe went back to his uncle's house in KwaMashu, and within a week he was able to secure a job in a Car Wash Company. He was very committed to his job, washing as many cars as he could in a day. And from the job, he managed to save up some money from the commission he was being paid for every car he washed. Then he went back to school to complete his High School education.

Sizwe passed Matric with six distinctions, and was admitted into the University of Johannesburg on government scholarship for a Bachelor's degree programme in Business Management.

After four years of full-time study at the
University of Johannesburg, Sizwe qualified
with distinction and was awarded a Bachelor
of Commerce degree in Business Management.

Sizwe was immediately employed as a
Manager by a multinational company
in Sandton.

After working in the company for one year, Sizwe enrolled for a part-time Master's degree programme in Business Management and he again qualified with distinction.

A few years later, Sizwe was promoted to the position of Executive Director. He was later appointed the Chief Executive Officer of the company.

It was now fifteen years since Sizwe kept his
envelope in a secret place in his uncle's house.
While he was on vacation he decided to go
there to open the envelope. Boldly written on
a piece of white paper inside the envelope was:
I want to be a Chief Executive Officer.

Sizwe gave thanks to his creator when he
discovered that his childhood dream had
actually come true.

After that, Sizwe drove from his uncle's house in KwaMashu to a Five-Star Hotel at the Durban beachfront where he had booked to spend his holidays with his wife and kids. As he parked his car at the front of the hotel, a man walked up to him and said, "Boss, I'm a famous car-guard here; I will look after your car nicely. I can also help you to wash the car for twenty rand (R20) if you don't mind." Sizwe turned to take a proper look at the man; it was Funani his schoolmate and childhood friend.

Sizwe was not happy to see his childhood friend and classmate in such a shameful condition, despite the virtuous counsel he offered him on the day he decided to quit street life.

At any rate, Sizwe advised Funani that there's no time too late for anyone to make a great life. There's always a time to pick up the pieces when all is not over, because where there's a will, there's always a way.

As we have learnt from this story, the **Golden Key** to Sizwe's successful life, against all odds, was his **ability** to use the **power of decision** – determination, self-discipline and effort – to redirect his focus in building his dream.

The moral of this story is that we are the master of our destiny. The person you are destined to become is the person you decide to be.

According to the American motivational author, Mark Victor Hansen, "What you think about comes about. By recording your dreams and goals on paper, you set in motion the process of becoming the person you most want to be."